Also by Ezra Jack Keats

The Little

PUFFIN BOOKS
Published by the Penguin Group
Penguin Putnam Books for Young Readers, 345 Hudson Street, New York, New York 10014, U.S.A.
Penguin Books Ltd, 27 Wrights Lane, London W8 5TZ, England

First published in the United States of America by The Macmillan Company, 1968
First published in Great Britain by The Bodley Head, 1969
Published by Viking and Puffin Books, divisions of Penguin Putnam Books for Young Readers, 2000

23

LIBRARY OF CONGRESS CATALOGING-IN-PUBLICATION DATA
Keats, Ezra Jack.
The little drummer boy / Ezra Jack Keats ; words and music by
Katherine Davis, Henry Onorati and Harry Simeone.
p. cm.
Originally published: The little drummer boy / Katherine Davis. New York : Macmillan, 1968.
Summary: An illustrated version of the Christmas carol about the
procession to Bethlehem and the offer of a poor boy to play his drum for
the Christ Child.
ISBN 0-670-89226-2 (hardcover) — ISBN 978-0-14-056743-4 (pbk.)
1. Carols, English—Texts. 2. Christmas music—Texts. [1. Carols. 2.
Christmas music.] I. Davis, Katherine, 1892- II. Onorati, Henry.
III. Simeone, Harry.
IV. Davis, Katherine, 1892- Little drummer boy. V. Title.
PZ8.3.K227 Li 2000
782.42'1723—dc21
00-008665

Manufactured in China.

Drummer Boy

EZRA JACK KEATS

Words and Music by Katherine Davis,
Henry Onorati and Harry Simeone

PUFFIN BOOKS

Come, they told me,
(pa-rum-pum-pum-pum)

Our newborn King to see,
(pa-rum-pum-pum-pum)

Our finest gifts to bring
(*pa-rum-pum-pum-pum*)

To lay before the King,
(*pa-rum-pum-pum-pum, rum-pum-pum-pum, rum-pum-pum-pum*)

So to honor Him
(*pa-rum-pum-pum-pum*)

When we come.

Baby Jesus,
(pa-rum-pum-pum-pum)

I am a poor boy too,
(pa-rum-pum-pum-pum)

I have no gift to bring
(pa-rum-pum-pum-pum)

That's fit to give a king,
(pa-rum-pum-pum-pum,
rum-pum-pum-pum,
rum-pum-pum-pum)

Shall I play for you
(pa-rum-pum-pum-pum)

On my drum?

Mary nodded,
(pa-rum-pum-pum-pum)

The ox and lamb kept time,
(pa-rum-pum-pum-pum)

I played my drum for Him,
(pa-rum-pum-pum-pum)

I played my best for Him,
(pa-rum-pum-pum-pum,
rum-pum-pum-pum,
rum-pum-pum-pum)

Then He smiled at me,
(pa-rum-pum-pum-pum)

Me and my drum.

The Little Drummer Boy

Words and Music by KATHERINE DAVIS, HENRY ONORATI and HARRY SIMEONE

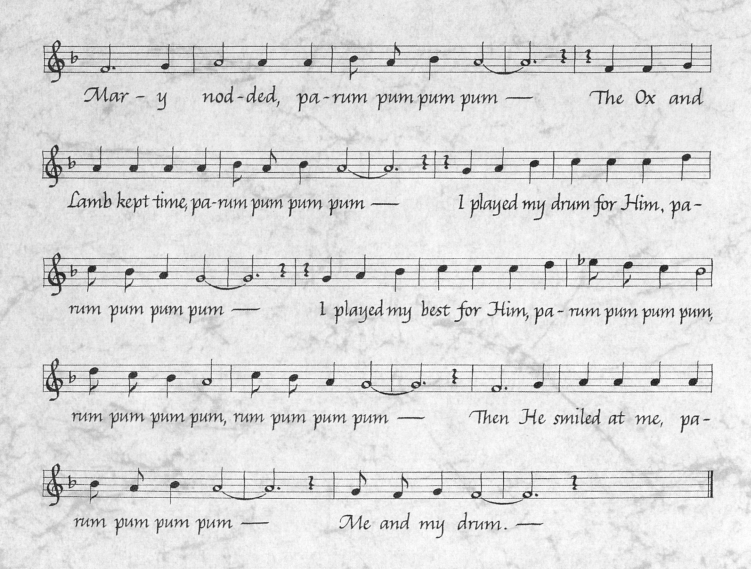

Mar - y   nod-ded, pa-rum pum pum pum —   The Ox and

Lamb kept time, pa-rum pum pum pum —   I played my drum for Him, pa-

rum pum pum pum —   I played my best for Him, pa-rum pum pum pum,

rum pum pum pum, rum pum pum pum —   Then He smiled at me, pa-

rum pum pum pum —   Me and my drum. —